The Mud House Mystery

by
Tony Savageau

Illustrated by
JoAnne Raditz

BLUE MUSTANG
P R E S S

Boston, Massachusetts

Library of Congress Control Number: 2001012345

ISBN: 0-9759737-0-3

PUBLISHED BY BLUE MUSTANG PRESS LLP
www.bluemustangpress.com
Boston, Massachusetts

Printed in the United States of America

The Wild Bunch

in

The Mud House Mystery

Mike –
I hope you enjoy
this story about a look
place in our hometown!
Happy Reading!

[signature]
Nov 24, 2004

For Thomas, William and Kelsie

Contents

ACKNOWLEDGEMENTS................9

CHAPTER 1 – The Kids................11

CHAPTER 2 – Lost!................17

CHAPTER 3 – Found!................23

CHAPTER 4 – What Has Six Sides?................29

CHAPTER 5 – The Mud House................35

CHAPTER 6 – A Bad Moon Rising................43

CHAPTER 7 – Star Struck................49

CHAPTER 8 – Here Comes The Sun................55

CHAPTER 9 – All Together Now................61

CHAPTER 10 – Unmasked................65

CHAPTER 11 – Tree House Tricks................71

CHAPTER 12 – Which Way Do We Go?................77

CHAPTER 13 – Zipping Along................83

CHAPTER 14 – Amazing................87

Acknowledgements

There are many people who helped me turn this story into a reality. Thanks to my wife, Karen, for editing and reviewing the many drafts of the *Mud House*. JoAnne, your illustrations help the story leap off the page and your editing helps the story to read easier, thank you. To Doreen and Kristin at Book Ends, I thank you for your unwavering support and encouragement for the Wild Bunch while simultaneously promoting reading and civic pride in our little town. To Miss Kitty and the MPL and their mission to ensure kids of all ages have the opportunity to read inside the walls of the library and to discover the world around them is only a few pages away. To the Juniors and Seniors of Mrs. Centrella and Mrs. DiSangro's class: your early appreciation, enthusiasm and support for the Wild Bunch are a constant reminder of why this is a fun thing for me to do. I'd also like to thank Donna and Doug Shephard who opened up their home to me as it became a central character in this story. And in general, to all the children from Massachusetts (my kids included), Texas, New Jersey and all places in between who've come up to me or written me letters about the fun and enjoyment they get from reading the Wild Bunch, I wouldn't be doing this if you guys didn't come up and say hello, so thank you! And, finally, to Mr. Bill: from Wolfratshausen to Bogenhausen, it's been a fun ride!

CHAPTER 1 – The Kids

"Joey! Take a look at this story in the newspaper," an excited Billy Wild shouted to his older brother. "Bernie's Cleaners was finally torn down yesterday. I guess Coach Joditz was right after all. And look, they even mention how we returned the Golden Skate to Mrs. Tolinsky."

Joey walked over to the kitchen table where his brother was reading the paper. Glancing over his little brother's shoulder to read the story himself, Joey could hardly believe how he, Billy, his sister Rose and their good friends the Roths had played such an important role in helping to solve that mystery. "That's pretty cool Billy. I feel kind of bad about Bernie's. We lost a proud old building there. At least we helped Mrs. Tolinsky reunite with her dad after being apart for so long. That was good. And to think after only a few short days of summer vacation, we've probably hit the high points already," Joey sighed.

"Watcha doin' boys?" Rose Wild asked as she came down the stairs of their home and made her way into the maple kitchen where the boys were reading the paper. Rose began looking for something to drink in the refrigerator.

"Not too much," Joey replied. "We're trying to think of something fun to do. Rose, do you have any ideas?"

"Hmmm. I don't know. Let me think for a second. We could help Mom and Dad with yardwork," offered Rose, while shaking her head *no* the whole time.

"Yeah, right," answered Billy, nose still firmly buried in the paper.

"Maybe we could see if the Joditz kids want to play," Rose said.

Joey thought about Rose's suggestion for a second. Then he said, "Good idea, Rose. Let's see if they're home. I'll tell Mom we're going down to their house." Joey stuck his head out the back door and yelled, "Mom! We're going over to Erick's house to see if they can play!"

"OK, but be back by six. The Joditz cookout starts then and we're going over there too," Mom said looking up from her vegetable garden. "And try to stay out of trouble, please! I don't want to come looking for you."

"We will, promise!" Joey said with a grin.

And with that, the Wild Bunch ran out of the front door. The kids walked down their driveway and crossed Colonial Drive to get to the sidewalk. As they passed the Tebold house, they saw Ronny Tebold mowing his lawn while his wife, Patty, was playing catch with little David. Rose asked, "Hi Patty, is Missy home?" Missy was Rose's best friend. Those two had a lot of fun together around the neighborhood.

"No, she's at a birthday party until later this afternoon," replied Patty.

"Rats!" exclaimed Rose. "Maybe I'll stop by later to play."

"OK, hunny," Mrs. Tebold said with a wave. "We'll be at the Joditz cookout later. We'll see you then."

"Perfect! I'll see you later!" Rose was happy.

Continuing down the sidewalk, the Wild Bunch passed the Cooper home. The kids noticed that it didn't look like anybody was home. Every year after school let out, the Coopers would spend their time at their summer house on the Cape. That left the neighborhood just a little bit emptier since the five of them could take up a lot room in a swimming pool or when everyone was playing games in the yard.

Next door at the Bleber house, Mr. and Mrs. Bleber were planting trees in their front yard. A big pile of mulch was sitting in the driveway just waiting to be spread around the yard. *They're going to have a big forest in their front yard before too long*, thought Joey.

By this time, the Wild Bunch had arrived at the Joditz house. Making their way up the steep, long driveway, they began to hear voices and laughter coming from the backyard. The Wilds walked past the garage and went around back to see what the commotion was all about.

Two of the three Joditz children were playing Bocce ball in the backyard. Erick was a year younger than Joey, but a year older than Billy, a very important distinction around the neighborhood. Roxie was a year younger than Billy: that was a key point from Billy's perspective. And playing on the swing set was the youngest Joditz child, Maryann. Maryann was a little more than a year younger than Rose. Between the six of them, they had six consecutive birth years covered from start to finish.

Coach and Mrs. Joditz were hanging out by their pool. Mr. Joditz was Erick and Joey's T-ball coach several years earlier. Coach Joditz's company, Calamity Demolition, had just completed tearing down Bernie's Cleaners a few days before. He was enjoying a much-deserved day off. Mrs. Joditz was busily sketching a picture poolside.

Joey called out, "Hey Erick, what are you guys up to today? Can you play?"

Erick dropped his Bocce ball on the grass and ran over to the Wilds. "Not much, we're just killing time. Do you guys want to do something?"

"Yeah. We thought you all might want to play baseball or something." Joey said.

Erick looked around and bent in close to Joey, so only the Wilds could hear. "Baseball is fine and all. You know I love playing baseball. But I've got another idea." Erick looked over to where his parents were sitting; glanced over his shoulder to make sure nobody else was listening in to his conversation. With a sly grin, he said, "I've got a secret fort in the woods not far from here. It's near an old, abandoned well. Nobody knows where it is but me. I've got a radio there and some tin cans we can string together and use as walkie-talkies. What do you say?"

The Wilds looked at each other and shrugged. "That sounds like a good plan to us. We have nothing better going on until the cookout," Joey replied.

Rose was trying to picture how in the world two tin cans could be used as walkie-talkies. She wondered where the batteries would go. Oh well, she was sure Erick knew what he was talking about.

"Cool. Hey Roxie, Maryann, come over here for a second." The girls ran over to where their big brother was having his meeting. "We're going to the fort I was telling you about to play with the Wilds. Go get some water and snacks. Hurry up."

The girls just stood there.

"So go on, why are you just standing there?" Erick asked.

"Erick, you're not the boss of us," Maryann said indignantly, while tapping her foot. "And you didn't even say *please*. But since it's for the Wilds, I'll go get the snacks." She ran into the house to get the supplies.

At this point, Mrs. Joditz took notice of the kids huddled

together whispering, like they had a big secret or something. "What are you kids cooking up now?"

Erick looked back and replied, "Nothing Mom. We're going to play in the woods with the Wilds for a little bit."

"OK, Erick. But you kids need to be back by supper time. We're having the neighbors over to celebrate Dad's fortieth birthday. There'll be lots of food, friends and neighbors coming over. Don't be late, please."

"No problem, Mom." Erick was smiling. He looked forward to playing in his secret fort in the woods. This was a secret he had yet to share with anyone. Erick was excited to be taking his sisters and the Wilds to his top secret fort.

Unfortunately for the Wild Bunch and the Joditz kids, they would never make it to Erick's fort on this summer day.

CHAPTER 2 – Lost!

Maryann met the rest of the kids out in the front yard. She had three water bottles and little packs of crackers everyone could share as they started their journey to find Erick's fort. Erick took the lead.

He led the children down his driveway and turned west onto Colonial. The group walked in this direction for about a quarter of a block. At the corner of Pilgrim Road, he crossed the street, after looking both ways, and began walking south. Rose asked, "How far away is this fort, Erick? If there even *is* a fort, she whispered to Maryann."

"It's not that far, we aren't even in the woods yet," Erick replied, shaking his head from side to side. Everyone continued walking down Pilgrim. After passing several houses, Erick stopped and looked around. He waved for everyone to gather around him. "OK, this is where we cut into the woods. Right between these two houses," Erick pointed over his shoulder. "Is everyone ready?"

Everyone nodded. Hands on hips, Maryann said, "Erick, what's the big deal, let's just get there. Nobody cares if this is a *secret* fort or not."

Erick just shook his head. His little sister didn't understand how important it was to protect the location of a *secret* fort. After all, if everyone knew about it, it wouldn't exactly be a *secret* fort anymore, right? It would be just a regular fort. Anyone could have a regular fort. Only he had a *secret* fort. "Let's go, one by one, into the woods. Wait for me just beyond the tree line. I don't want to attract any attention," Erick instructed.

"What's a tree line?" Rose asked.

Erick looked at Rose, a look of surprise on his face. "You don't know what a tree line is?"

"Nope", Rose replied.

"Me either," Roxie joined in.

"Oh brother…" Erick moaned. "It's where the backyard stops and the trees begin. It's right there, do you see it? That's a tree line."

The girls looked over to where Erick was pointing.

"Yeah, we see it Erick. Why didn't you just say that in the first place?" Maryann asked, eyebrows raised and hands spread wide, shoulders in a shrug.

Exasperated, Erick shook his head and said, "OK, OK. You're right, it's my fault you two didn't understand me in the first place. Now that we all know what a tree line is, can we please go?"

"Sure," Roxie said, "what's the big deal? And you did say please. Let's go then." Roxie was smiling.

One by one, and on Erick's signal, the Wild Bunch and the Joditz kids ran into the woods. Erick was the last to slip into the woods between the houses. Everyone was there waiting for him, just beyond the now famous tree line.

Billy thought being in these woods must be a lot like life had been when the English colonists first ventured into this area of Massachusetts to explore the great Hockomock Swamp over 325 years ago. He had learned about the swamp in Ms. Zeedman's third grade class last year at the Jordan school. Billy wondered to himself if the English colonists had ever run into the legendary Bigfoot while exploring these woods. Although he wasn't sure Bigfoot had ever been seen this far east, he thought it could be possible. Anything was possible. He figured Bigfoot's family probably started their family here too, just like the English. And when it got too crowded the Bigfoot family packed up and moved west like everyone else did. As Billy daydreamed about how he would look in colonial clothing, standing next to Bigfoot, Erick interrupted his thought.

"OK, now that we're in the woods, we go over this way." Erick led them down what looked like a very narrow path. The path was probably used by the deer Erick occasionally observed very early in the mornings from his bedroom window. During the day, the deer disappeared deep into the woods until all the people went to sleep. When it was safe to come out of the woods, the deer ate his mom's hosta plants and flowers. His mom didn't think that was too cool. But the deer have to eat Erick reasoned.

The ground was covered with small blueberry bushes while scrubby, scraggly oak trees towered above the group. Oak and pine trees were thick in this part of the woods. There were so many rocks and boulders covering the ground, one wondered how any plant or tree could possibly grow. In fact, some of the trees grew right out of the rocks. The group continued walking down hill and without warning, the path disappeared.

Erick paused for a moment, pointed to the right and said, "Follow me."

The group followed Erick's lead. However, the going was much rougher now. There was no path. The rocks were everywhere and the slope of the hill was getting steeper. Joey said, "Hey Erick, are we going uphill now? How much farther is the fort?"

"Yeah," Maryann said, "I think Rose was right. I'll bet you there's not a single *secret* fort in these woods."

"Oh no, there's a fort all right. We're very close. Just a few more minutes," Erick reassured them. "Let's rest here on this rock and have a drink of water and eat some of the crackers." Erick was standing in front of a big flat rock.

"Good idea!" Roxie exclaimed.

The kids stopped and jumped onto the large boulder in the middle of the woods. All around them, they saw trees and rocks, rocks and trees. No houses were visible from their resting place. They shared the water and the crackers Maryann packed for them at the beginning of their journey.

After a brief rest, Erick gathered the group up and urged them to continue forward. Now it appeared they were heading downhill. Slipping on the rocks, they saw what looked like a small creek ahead. The land was turning very marshy and moist. Rose noticed lots of moss on the trees too. Billy heard frogs calling out. *Ribbit. Ribbit.*

Erick was suddenly very quiet. He stopped walking. He turned around. He hesitated for a moment and then announced, "OK, you're probably wondering where my fort is." Erick looked around the woods. "I have to admit. I'm wondering the same thing. I have no idea where we are. I hate to say this…but we're lost."

"Lost!" Billy exclaimed. "How can we be lost?"

Sullenly, Erick replied, "I don't know. We just are. I've only been to my fort one time before today. Everything looks the same out here in the woods. I could have sworn my fort was right over there. But it's not."

At that precise moment, everyone turned their heads. A loud crashing noise came from behind a long line of big bushes, just off to their right.

Billy yelled, "Bigfoot!"

Everybody screamed.

CHAPTER 3 – Found?

"Wait, wait, wait," Joey said. "Everybody calm down a second. Billy's been reading too many stories again. Bigfoot doesn't live around here anymore. He lives on the West Coast." And with that calm reassurance, the kids relaxed. But suddenly, another crashing sound off to their left caused them to turn in that direction. Finally, they saw movement. Whatever made that noise began to reveal itself.

Something in that line of bushes moved toward them, ever so slowly. Whatever *it* was, was now more cautious than before. More deliberate. Billy imagined *it* was like a lion stalking its dinner or, despite what Joey said, *it* was a member of a Bigfoot family left behind hundreds of years ago to protect these woods. Branches snapped as *it* moved closer and closer to the group. All at once, the bushes shook to and fro, back and forth in a furious flurry of leaves, berries and twigs!

Suddenly, out from under a big blueberry bush, *it* came into view. *It* was like nothing the kids had imagined. Looks of fear and foreboding spread across their faces. *It* was a big…bad…*SKUNK*! A big old skunk ambled slowly in their direction. Now, this skunk was only about as big as a cat, but by now the kids' imaginations were running wild. It seemed to them this skunk was as big as a Dalmation or maybe even a horse.

Billy yelled, "Bigskunk!"

"Don't anyone move a muscle," Joey said. "If we stand still, maybe he'll leave us alone."

The skunk was about twenty feet away from where the kids had gathered. He sniffed and nibbled blueberries off the bushes. He paused for a second and looked their way. Skunks can't see very well, after all. He sniffed the air. He squinted in the kids' direction once again. He raised his tail and it started twitching. The kids held their breath, hoping beyond hope they wouldn't get sprayed by a skunk in these woods.

Roxie remembered back to when a skunk fell into their pool a few years ago. The skunk had a hard time getting out and in its panic, it sprayed the pool. Everything smelled like skunk for weeks, it was not very pleasant.

The skunk's tail twitched some more. Then, without warning, he lowered his tail, turned around and slowly waddled off in the direction from which he had come.

"Whew, that was a close one," Billy said. "It was bad enough that skunk was the size of Bigfoot and could have eaten us for lunch, but he might have sprayed us too."

"Billy, that skunk was about the size of our cat," Joey said. "Besides, they have pretty poor eyesight; he probably didn't even notice we were standing in front of him."

"I don't know, Joey, he looked pretty big to me," Billy said.

"Boys! Who cares how big the skunk was? Erick just said we are lost. Did anyone else hear him say that? What do we do now? I want to go home." Rose said.

"Me too," Maryann added in a soft voice.

"Hang on everybody. We haven't been walking for very long. We can't be too far from home. Let's cross over that creek and see what's beyond that big rock," Joey was trying to be brave and reassure everyone. He was the oldest after all.

The children made their way towards the creek. Once they made it to the edge of the creek, Joey found a couple of big rocks and threw them into the middle of the creek to serve as stepping-stones. One by one, the kids crossed the shallow creek over to the other side. Many minutes later, Joey, now leading the way, held up his hand so the others would stop.

"I think I see a clearing up ahead. Erick, you come with me. Billy you stay here with the girls and make sure everybody is OK. Don't go anywhere. We'll be right back after we figure out what is up there."

"But Joey, I don't want to stay with…" Billy began to protest. He saw Joey shoot him a look he knew meant for him to be quiet. "…OK, we'll be right here. Roxie, can I have another drink, please?"

Erick, who was feeling bad about getting the group lost, was grateful Joey asked him to come along to help investigate. "Thanks, Joey. I'm sorry I got all of us lost."

"Don't worry about it, Erick. These woods are tricky. Everything starts to look the same after a while. We'll figure this out together. It's no problem, really."

Joey and Erick made their way towards the clearing. Moving slowly, they hiked through the stinging nettles and heavy underbrush. Suddenly, they found themselves standing behind a metal structure. Joey cleared a few branches away. Sure enough, they were standing behind a barrier about three feet high. It was the same kind of barrier used to keep cars from crashing off the road. There was something funny about this barrier though. It was painted a camouflage color. It wasn't silver like most barriers you see along a road or those you see protecting a bridge. The barrier blended in perfectly with the surrounding woods. *This looks familiar, but I can't quite place it*, Joey thought. *Where have I seen this before? This barrier is very hard to see because it blends in so well, but there's something about it.*

Looking over the barrier, the boys saw a small, two-lane asphalt road in front of them. Joey turned to say something to Erick when he jumped, startled. Standing right behind them were the other kids, Billy in the lead. They had followed them to the barrier after all. "I thought I told you to stay back there and wait for word from us," Joey whispered, pointing over the kids' heads.

Rose whispered back, "We didn't want to. Billy said Bigskunk might still want to spray us."

Joey looked at Billy and shook his head. "Bigskunk? So now we have the legendary Mansfield Bigskunk?"

Billy just looked at Joey.

"Never mind Billy, you guys are here, I'm glad you followed us. It will save us some time. Come up here and take a look. It's a road."

"I'll bet people would come from miles around just to see the Mansfield Bigskunk," Billy mumbled to himself.

The remaining four kids made their way to the barrier to take a look. "Yep, it's a road all right," Roxie said. "And roads lead to somewhere. Hopefully this road leads to home."

Everyone was looking at the road except for Maryann. Maryann was pointing off to the right, across the street and up a lonely dirt road. "I see a castle," she said.

Erick answered, "Don't be silly, Maryann, there are no castles in Mansfield. It's an old town, but not that old."

"Then what is that?" Rose asked, pointing in the same direction as Maryann.

Everyone turned to look where the youngest children were pointing. Sure enough, up the dirt road, and up on a hill was a pinkish colored building that looked almost, but not quite, round.

"What in the world is that?" Billy wondered.

"Wow! A castle right here in town. I never knew we had castles here. But I do know one thing," Erick replied.

"What's that?" Maryann asked.

"It's not my fort," Erick answered. "And I think that means we're still lost."

"Maybe we can call Mom to come pick us up from there," Roxie said hopefully. "Wherever *there* is."

"Good idea," Joey said, once again taking charge. "Let's jump over this barrier and see if anyone's home."

Everyone hopped over the barrier, was careful to look both ways, and then crossed the little two-lane road.

The Wild Bunch noticed the dirt road leading up to the castle was longer than it looked from behind the barrier.

What they didn't notice was somebody lying on their belly on the roof of the castle. That somebody was studying them intently. Watching every move they made as they trudged up the dirt road. That somebody had an ominous smile on their face.

The day that had started out to be such a normal day, was about to become much more interesting.

CHAPTER 4 – What Has Six Sides?

"How long is this road, anyway?" Rose complained. "It seems like we've been walking forever."

"Just a few more yards," Joey replied. "I can see the castle just up ahead."

The Wild Bunch and the Joditz kids heard a strange noise as they made their way up the hill. Joey held up his hand and everyone stopped walking.

"Shhhhh. Do you hear that?" Joey asked.

"Yeah, I hear it," Erick replied.

"Me too," Rose said.

"It sounds like clucking to me," Roxie offered.

"I think you're right. It is clucking. Let's keep going," Joey waved the group forward.

As the group continued up the road, a chicken ran past them towards what looked like an old garage, or maybe it was a barn, and then the chicken disappeared behind the building. The kids jumped back as the bird crossed their path.

"Well, we have confirmed a chicken is making the clucking noise. And it's a scrawny chicken at that. What would a chicken be doing on the grounds of a castle?" Billy wondered.

"Maybe it's a watch-chicken, you know, instead of a watch-dog?" Rose offered.

"It could be, but you'd think whoever owns this castle would have a real dog to stand guard. Or maybe even a moat to keep out unwanted guests," Roxie reasoned.

"I'd hate to think of us as *unwanted* guests," Joey said. "Who wouldn't want us to stop by for a visit? I see some steps and the front door right over there. Let's see if anyone's home. Maybe we can use their phone to call for a ride."

"Good idea. The sooner the better," said Billy, who was still trying to get over his encounter with Bigskunk. Finding a castle with chickens also seemed out of place to him. He was getting a weird feeling.

The kids climbed the ivy covered steps and made their way to the front door. Joey was about to knock when he noticed the door was slightly ajar. He knocked anyway and called out, "Hello, is anyone home?" There was no reply. Joey looked around the big yard behind him, then turned and knocked again, "Helloooo." Still nothing. "It doesn't look like anyone's home. Let's walk around back and see if anybody's back there."

"Sounds good to me," Erick replied.

The Wild Bunch and the Joditz kids walked down the steps and around the pink castle. They crossed over a brick walkway between the castle and the barn. The walkway looked very old. Billy looked closely at the red bricks that made up the walkway. He noticed the bricks were stamped with the initials WWCo. He wondered what that meant. But he didn't want to stop and fall behind the others, so he moved on to catch up to the group.

"This house is shaped like a circle," Maryann remarked.

"Almost," Joey said. "But you see, the outside walls are in straight lines. More like some sort of polygon than a circle."

"I know what a polygon is," Billy said proudly. "We learned

about those in Ms. Zeedman's class. A polygon is a multi-sided object."

"Very good, Mr. Math-man, but it's not helping us get home," a worried Erick replied.

Joey continued, "And here we are, back where we started. I counted six sides to this castle. That makes it a…"

"Hexagon!" Billy shouted with a big smile on his face.

"Yes, a hexagon. And there was nobody around back either," Joey pondered the situation.

"Hey Joey, what's this note say?" Rose asked, as she pointed to a note that was tacked to the front door.

"Note? I didn't see this note before, did any of you?" Joey asked.

Head shakes *no* from everyone.

Joey took the note off the door. Joey read the note out loud so everyone could hear:

Lost and looking for your home?
The Mud House is the place to roam.
North? South? Which way to go?
It's for you to guess and me to know.

The answer you seek is in the book.
It won't take you long, have a look.
So come inside, and stop your talking,
And let your fingers do the walking.

"Let your fingers do the walking?" Maryann asked with a bewildered look on her face. "What does that mean? Who walks with their fingers? I can walk on my hands though. Watch." And with that, Maryann began walking around the front yard on her hands. And she did that quite well too.

"Maryann, stop showing off," Erick said impatiently. "I don't like the tone of this note. It sounds spooky. And I want to go home."

"The note must be a clue," Joey speculated. "Let your fingers do the walking. Mud House? Book? Hmmm. Sign language? A library? A Map? But if whoever wrote this note knew we were lost, why didn't they just come over and talk to us? Why leave this riddle for cryin' out loud?"

"Maybe they are shy," Rose offered.

Billy jumped into the conversation, "Erik's right. We've got to find our way home. The note says the answer is in the book. What book? It must be inside the house. What choice do we have?"

Joey responded, "Well, we can go into the house or we can try to find some help along that road we crossed to get here. I'm going to put it to a vote. Everyone who wants to go inside and find the book and the possible answer, or maybe just a phone, raise your hand."

Erick, Billy, and Rose raised their hands.

"Everyone who wants to continue along this road, raise your hands."

Joey, Roxie, and Maryann raised their hands.

"Great, we've got a tie!" Erick said. "How do we break the tie?"

Pulling a coin from his pocket, Joey said, "By using a time honored tradition. Heads we go inside. Tails we go back to the road and keep walking until we find help." Joey flipped the coin.

Everyone gathered around Joey as he caught the coin with his right hand and slapped it onto the top of his left hand. He uncovered the quarter. "Heads. We go inside." Joey stuffed the riddle into his pants pocket.

The kids couldn't see it, but now the mysterious figure was peeking out from behind the barn, watching them debate. The figure smiled a wicked smile.

CHAPTER 5 – The Mud House

Joey and the rest of the kids walked back up the steps to the front door. The front door was now completely closed. He knocked on the door again and waited. Nobody came to the door. Joey knocked again. Still nothing. As he put his ear to the door and listened for signs of life, the door slowly swung open. Joey looked at the kids gathered around him. They looked back at him, expectantly. Finally...

"Are we going in or what?" Rose prodded. "Let's find what we're looking for and get out of here."

"What, exactly, are we looking for?" Roxie asked.

Joey thought for a moment and replied, "The book. We've got to find that book. That book must have a map in it or something."

With that, the Wild Bunch and the Joditz kids walked through the front door.

They found themselves in a small foyer, shaped like a slice of pie. There was a picture on one wall with what looked like a painting of a family. Under the picture was a small card with some writing on it, much like you would see in a museum. Billy thought this was strange, especially for a home, assuming this was a home. There were three doors leading from the foyer to the interior of the house. A door on the left had a full moon painted on it, a door on the right had a five pointed star and the door at the end of the pie shaped room, opposite the front door, had a picture of the sun.

"Hello," Joey called out. "Is anyone home?"

There was no answer.

The kids began to fan out around the foyer to look around.

Joey walked up to the painting and studied it for a second. There were seven people in the painting. Three adults and four children were arranged in a traditional enough looking pose. Everyone was seated except for two small children. The little boy seated to the far left was holding a book. He was smiling. The lone woman in the middle of the picture was holding a baby. And in the background of the painting was the very house they were standing in. That was strange. To be looking at a picture of the house while they were *in* the house. Joey looked at the card. "Hey guys, listen to this:

This is a painting by George Stearns of the William Stearns family in the Hexagon (Mud) House. George and Orange Scott Stearns built the house in 1855. Later a barn was added. George Stearns (1826 – 1902) was a noted painter, preacher, and builder of the Mud House. Orange Stearns (1835 – 1870) enlisted in Company G of the 29th Regiment of Massachusetts Volunteers in 1861."

The other kids had drifted over to the painting while Joey was reading. After reading the card, Joey turned to face the group.

"That's why the barrier looked familiar!" Joey exclaimed while snapping his fingers.

"Why's that, Joey?" Erick asked.

"I'm pretty sure the road out there is Stearns Avenue. It must have been named after the family that built this very house. We used to live on this street when we first moved to Mansfield.

When Billy was little, Mom and Dad would push us in a double stroller up and down this road. I was little, but I do remember that barrier now."

"Great, you know the street name, Joey, so what?" a worried Erick said.

"Well, now I know how to get home! Colonial runs into Stearns about a half mile or so up the hill."

"Really? Then what are we waiting for? Let's get out of here and get home." Erick was less worried now.

"She looks kind of pretty," Rose said about the woman in the picture as she wandered over to take a look. "I wonder what the baby's name was."

"Nobody's really smiling all that much, except for the lady holding the book," Billy noticed. "I wonder if they were happy to have their picture painted. It takes a long time to paint a picture."

"Maybe they aren't smiling because they had to go to the bathroom," Maryann reasoned. "That would take my smile away too."

Roxie leaned in to get a better look at the painting. "Hey Joey, did you happen to notice the woman in the middle is holding a book? Do you think it's the same book from the note on the front door?"

Joey looked at Roxie and Billy with a confused look on his face. "Roxie, the little boy on the left is holding the book. The lady in the middle is holding the baby. I mean, look right here…" Joey turned to face the painting again. He stopped in mid-sentence. The color drained from his face. He opened his mouth, but at first, nothing came out. He shook his head in disbelief. But there it was. Plain as the day is long. The little boy he could have sworn was holding the book just a few seconds ago was now holding the baby. He was no longer smiling. The lady in the middle of the portrait was holding the book up with both of her hands, smiling. Joey spun back to face the kids. Joey's quick turn startled the others and they all looked at him.

"I promise you guys," Joey said, "that lady was holding the baby just before you came over here. Now she's holding the book. I must be going crazy."

Rose was pointing to the painting. "I don't think so, Joey. Look now."

Slowly, Joey turned to face the painting again. His eyes were closed. He was afraid of what he might see now. The other kids shifted their gaze from Joey back to the painting. There was a collective gasp. Joey opened his eyes.

Now, the man to the far right was standing up with the book in his right hand. He was not smiling. He had a sad look on his face and was pointing at the book. The lady no longer had the book or the baby. Her smile was gone. The other adult male in the picture was now holding the baby. He wasn't smiling either. And the little boy who had the book the first time looked like he might be crying. Everyone in the painting seemed to be looking right at the Wild Bunch and the Joditz kids. It was unsettling.

With a worried, forced smile, Erick said, "I think they are trying to tell us something. So…let's go home, OK? This is a little too weird for me."

Joey gathered the group around him into a huddle. "Erick, I know we all want to get home. But something is going on here. The people in the painting are trying to tell us something. They look sad. It must have to do with the book."

Everyone turned to look at the painting again. By now, they were used to the painting changing on them and were only slightly less surprised this time when it changed again. Everyone in the painting was exactly the same as when Joey first saw the painting, but with one big difference. There was no book to be seen anywhere in the picture. It was gone!

Joey spoke, "That seals it. It's the book. They want us to find that book. Maybe it just *belongs* here in the house or something."

"But I don't see the book anywhere in here. Do you think it is behind one of these three doors?" Roxie wondered aloud. "I wonder which one?"

"I'm not sure which door leads to the book, or even if they lead to the book. But I do have an idea," Joey said. "Let's split up two by two. Each pair will pick a door until we find the book. This house can't be that big, it shouldn't take too long."

The other kids looked at each other and nodded their agreement. This sounded like a pretty good plan to them. Except for Erick, he didn't like this at all.

"I want to go home. And you're not going to stop me," Erick said as he made his way back to the front door. He grabbed the doorknob and turned. Nothing. He pulled harder. Nothing. The door wouldn't budge. Erick wasn't going out that way.

"OK. Maybe we do it your way, Joey. What have we got to lose?" Erick smiled weakly as he turned to face the group.

Joey nodded.

"But who is going to go with whom?" Rose asked.

"Well, let's figure that out now, OK?" Joey replied. Since I'm the oldest one here, I'll go with Maryann since she's the youngest. Erick, you're the second oldest and a black belt in karate, so you go with Rose. Billy, you're a karate brown belt, so you and Roxie can look out for each other. Does that sound fair?"

Everyone again, nodded their agreement. These were good pairings. Everybody was comfortable with this set up.

Joey said, "To decide which doors we go through, let's do rock, paper, scissors. Erick and I will go first. Ready? Rock, paper, scissors, shoot."

When Joey said shoot, Erick finished with the scissor sign while Joey came up paper. "Scissors cut paper, I win!" Erick said excitedly.

"OK, Erick, which door do you want?"

"I'll shoot for the moon!" Erick said, chuckling.

"OK. Erick and Rose will take the moon door. Billy, are you ready?"

Billy nodded.

"Rock, paper, scissors, shoot!"

Billy made the paper sign while Joey came up rock. "Paper covers rock, I get to pick," Billy said. "Roxie and I will catch a rising star."

"OK, that seals it, Maryann and I will follow the sun. Ready to go little darlin'?" Joey asked.

Rose was shaking her head when she said, "You boys took all that time to figure that out by playing the paper, rock, shoot game? Boys!"

"Hey, it was the only fair way," Joey said, defending his method. "Now, if you don't find the book in ten minutes or so, we'll meet back here, got it?"

"Ten minutes, got it," Erick said.

"Yep, 600 seconds, and we'll be back," Billy said.

"Great, then let's go team! Let's find that book!"

And with that, each pair stepped to their respective doors, opened them and walked through, closing the doors behind them. Within seconds, the mysterious figure came through the front door holding a skeleton key. The figure had unlocked the front door with his key. The mystery shadow calmly walked up to each door, inserted the key, and turned the key to lock the door. The figure locked every door behind each pair of kids. The mysterious person let out a spooky chuckle and smiled. And with a glance at the painting hanging on the wall, the figure turned and went back out the front door.

Nobody in the painting was smiling. In fact, looks of concern spread across their faces. The Stearns family looked worried.

CHAPTER 6 – A Bad Moon Rising

"Ummm, Erick, did you just hear a clicking sound coming from our door?" Rose asked.

"What click? What are you talking about Rose?"

"I just heard a click after I shut the door." Turning back to the door, Rose tried the knob, it wouldn't turn. "I don't think we're going to get back to the foyer through this door Erick, it's locked."

"Locked!" Erick exclaimed. "You must be wrong, let me try." Erick jiggled the door, tugged at the knob, nothing. They were trapped! "You're right, Rose, we're locked in."

"I told you that, a minute ago," Rose said, rolling her eyes. "Why didn't you believe me? So what do you want to do?"

"Let's see if we can find the book and get out of here. This place is really starting to creep me out."

Rose and Erick turned away from the door and faced the room. The room was in a pie shape like the foyer, but was about twice as big as the entry way. There were pictures of moons hanging on every wall. The walls were a dark blue, almost black, and it sort of looked like nighttime in the room. There were moon lamps and furniture with moons on them. There was even a moon alarm clock, ticking in the corner of the room. An old radio with a moon shaped hole cut into it. They looked all around. The one thing they didn't see was the book.

Erick walked over to the window. The window looked out over the driveway they all had walked up earlier. He tried to open the window, which was framed with moon curtains, but it wouldn't budge. He banged on the window a couple of times, but to no avail. He noticed a card in the window with some writing on it and picked it up. The card said George Stearns' father was a guy named Issac, who was apparently well known in Mansfield. It said Issac was a school teacher, newspaper writer and a publisher. He was also an avid reader and loved books. *Interesting*, Erick thought, *but it's not going to help me get home*.

Rose walked over to the clock. She was staring at it. As she continued staring at it, she wrinkled her nose. Something about the clock was not quite right, but she wasn't sure what exactly it was that was making her feel that way.

"Hey Erick, come over here for a second and look at this clock. Something's wrong with it, but I'm not sure what it is."

Erick wandered over and let out a heavy sigh. He did not want to look at some dumb old clock. He wanted to find the book so he could finally go home. He looked at the clock and stared. Erick couldn't take his eyes off of the clock either. Finally, it dawned on him what was so fascinating about this strange clock.

"Rose, the clock is running backwards."

"Backwards?"

"Yes, backwards. Watch the second hand. It's going the wrong way."

"Oh yeah, would you look at that? You're absolutely right. Who would want a clock running backwards? You'd always be early." Rose remarked.

"That's what I have been doing, Rose. *Looking* at that clock. For some reason, I can't stop looking at it."

Rose shook her head to clear it and walked away from the clock. Erick was still staring at it when she clicked on the radio.

Music began to play. Erick walked over and listened.

"Man, that's an old radio. I'm surprised it still plays. Everything seems a little old in here, don't you think?"

"Maybe. Listen to that music. It sounds…so…strange, too. Do you know any of these songs?"

Erick listened closely. He began to shake his head. "Yeah, maybe. It sounds like some real old stuff my parents listen to sometimes. From the 80's, I think. It is real, real old. I can't understand how they enjoy listening to this stuff."

"Erick, this old radio is playing real old music. The clock is running backwards. Do you think we've gone backwards in time?"

"Back in time?"

"Yeah, when we stepped through that door, maybe we went back in time!" Rose was starting to worry now.

Erick began to feel the panic well up through his body. He thought back to his black belt training and took a deep breath. He didn't want Rose to worry. He had to calm himself and be strong, for the both of them.

"No, Rose. I don't think so. Let's keep looking around. We'll find that book or at least another way out. You'll see." Erick didn't quite believe what he was saying, but he was pleased to see his little speech calmed Rose down. The kids continued to explore the nooks and crannies of the room. Rose was behind the moon covered couch, feeling around the wall when she felt the wall give, just a little bit.

"Hey Erick, come over here."

"Now what is it, Rose?"

"Push on this wall with me, it moves."

Erick added his weight to Rose's and they pushed the wall together. Slowly, it began to move and swung inward. Erick could see that small hinges allowing the door to move were covered up by the dark paint. This was a door. The kids were looking at a secret door with no door knob. They'd found a door hidden behind the moon couch in this strange moon room.

Peering into the opening, "It looks like a tunnel or something," Rose commented.

"It sure does. Hey look, here's a switch." Erick flipped the switch and a set of lights hanging from the middle of the tunnel's ceiling flickered on as far down the opening as the eye could see.

Erick and Rose looked at each other. They looked back to the locked moon door and shrugged their shoulders.

"Rose, we've got no choice. This is the only way out of the room. There's no book in here. We've got to check it out and see if this leads us to the book."

"OK, Erick, if you say so. But what do you think is down there?"

"Well, there's only one way to find out. Let's go."

Erick took Rose's hand and they began their journey down the tunnel. The walls were mostly earth and rocks, but shored up with old concrete and large wooden beams. It smelled musty, like a basement, but older and more dank. After walking for a minute or two, although it seemed much longer, they came to a set of stairs leading up to a cellar bulkhead. The two kids looked at each other and walked up the steps, slowly, very slowly. When they reached the bulkhead, Erick pushed on the door. It opened. The kids stuck their heads carefully out of the bulkhead and looked around.

"Oh, my goodness...what is this place?" Rose asked in an astonished whisper.

Then there was silence.

CHAPTER 7 – Star Struck

At almost the same time as Erick and Rose discovered they were locked in the moon room, Roxie made her own disturbing discovery in the star room. "It won't budge, Billy. Somebody just locked this door behind us and we can't get out." Roxie was very concerned.

Billy tried the door himself. Sure enough, they were locked in. "Well, there's not much we can do about it now, let's see if we can find the book and maybe then we can go home."

Billy and Roxie surveyed the room. Although the kids couldn't know this, the star room was almost the same size as the moon room. The ceiling was much higher than in a regular room, at least 15 feet high. The room was almost completely bare and painted solid white. Hanging from the ceiling were dozens of shining stars, almost like you'd find atop a Christmas tree. There was a big star painted in the center of the room and one entire wall was painted with little stars that seemed to be twinkling. There were a few windows, high up near the ceiling that let most of the light spill into the center of the room.

It was an incredibly bright white light that warmed the room. As Billy looked more closely, he discovered there were at least five star shaped windows allowing the light to stream into the room from the outside. There were star shaped chairs and star shaped rugs on the painted wood floor that was covered in, you guessed it, stars. Pictures of stars were hanging on the walls in frames and stars turned every piece of furniture into a starry resting place.

"Now if this room can't brighten your day, nothing will," Roxie remarked.

"You've got that right, Roxie. Have you ever seen so many stars in one room?

"Never. Although my classroom at the Jackson school had a wall of various shapes on it, there were more than stars to go around. There was nothing like this at all. This is a very different place."

"Do you see any books lying around? A star shaped book maybe?"

Roxie laughed. "Not yet, but let's keep looking."

"I don't see anything, Roxie. No books, no TV, no stereo, only this weird thing."

Walking over to where Billy stood, "Roxie peered over his shoulder. "Oh, Billy, that's an old telescope."

"I guess in some way, that makes sense for this room. If you want to gaze at the stars, you would need a telescope," Billy commented. "I wonder what I can see when I look through it." Billy pulled the telescope closer to one of the star windows.

Billy positioned the telescope just so and looked through the eyepiece. He stood up with a funny look on his face. Billy shook his head as if to clear it. He peered in the direction the telescope was pointed, changed position slightly and looked through the eyepiece again. Much to his surprise, he saw the same thing. Billy was looking at a book. Billy saw the book through the telescope! He pointed the telescope into the room, towards Roxie and looked again, expecting to see Roxie's nose about 20 times too big. But Billy didn't see her nose, he saw the book!

"Roxie, check this out! No matter where I point this

telescope, all I see is the book. I can't explain it. I'm positive this is the book from the painting."

Roxie came over to take a look for herself. She looked through the eyepiece and, sure enough, she saw the book too. "But Billy, the telescope is showing us the book, but we can't see it without the telescope. Where is the book then?"

"I'm not sure. I can't figure it out. But I noticed this when I was moving the telescope around." Billy was pointing towards the floor.

"Is that a handle under the rug?" Roxie asked.

Billy and Roxie walked over for a closer look. Billy looked at Roxie. "Why don't you push the rug aside and see what's under there."

"Wait a minute buster, you are the oldest and your brother put you in charge because you're the karate expert. You move it."

Billy couldn't argue with Roxie's logic, plus, he didn't want to appear afraid in front of a girl younger than he was, even if she could do everything as well as he could. So, he dropped into the left-guard position and with tip of his toe, began lifting the rug off the floor. Slowly, very slowly, the rug pulled away. Underneath it was what could only be described as a trap door with a small iron ring for a handle.

"What do you suppose that is?" Roxie asked.

"It's a door to someplace else. But where is someplace else? And do we want to go there?"

"Billy, I really don't know. We haven't found the book, the door we came in is locked and I don't see any other way out of here. We've got to try it."

"Yeah, you're right. Give me a hand, please."

Together, Billy and Roxie pulled on the ring and opened the trap door the rest of the way. The star-shaped hole led down into a corridor of some sort. There was a small ladder, but it was very dark down there and hard to see.

"There's not much light down there, Roxie. I don't know about this."

Roxie looked around the room. She smiled and ran over to a table near the door they entered the room from. On the table was a flashlight, with the light shaped as, what else, a star. She grabbed the flashlight and ran back to Billy.

"Here we go, let's take a little of this star light with us then."

"OK, you hold the light on me as I go down the ladder, then drop the light down to me and I'll beam it up as you come down."

"Sounds like a plan to me."

Billy made his way down the short ladder while Roxie held the light on him. She dropped the flashlight down to Billy and he shined the light up at her while she made her way down. When they turned around and shined the light down the corridor, all they could see was darkness. The corridor was finished, and seemed much newer than the rest of the house. As they walked down the corridor, they noticed water dripping here and there and heard what sounded like small animals scurrying out of their way. They were both afraid, but they pressed on.

Soon, they found themselves at the end of the corridor facing another small ladder that led up to a trap door that was identical to the one they climbed down a few minutes before.

"Roxie, hold the light and shine it up at me while I go up and see if the door will open."

Roxie shined the light up at Billy as he scrambled up the ladder and pushed up on the trap door. It began to open. He opened it all the way, climbed out into another room and had Roxie toss the light up to him. He shined the light down at her while she climbed up the ladder. Roxie hopped out of the trap door onto the floor. The kids brushed themselves off and turned around.

"Roxie, we're not in the star room anymore," Billy remarked.

They certainly were not. It was as if Billy and Roxie had discovered a whole new world.

CHAPTER 8 – Here Comes The Sun

As the others struggled to understand their discoveries Joey Wild turned to face the young Maryann, "You're right Maryann, the door is locked. I wonder how that happened. I guess we'll be going out a different way than we came in. Don't worry though, we'll figure it out together. OK, let's take a look around and see if that book is in here."

When the kids turned around, they did not see a room right away like the others had seen. Instead, they saw a staircase leading up to the second floor. "Oh no, not again," Joey remarked. He was thinking back to the staircase at Bernie's he had climbed several days before with his siblings. It was at the top of those stairs he had found something that led to the Wild Bunch's first adventure of the summer.

"What was that you said, Joey?" Maryann asked.

"Oh, it's nothing. I was just thinking about someplace else that looked a lot like this does. It's nothing. Let's head up and see what's in store for us." Joey and Maryann began climbing the stairs.

At the top of the stairs, they found themselves in a large room painted yellow. The yellow had a golden hue to it, almost like the color of honey. This room was about the size of two or three of the pie shaped rooms on the first floor. Windows all around the top of the high, high ceiling that must have been the roof, although it was hard to tell from inside the house. Joey couldn't imagine there being another floor on top of this one.

Curiously, about ten feet off the floor was what looked like an overhang or ledge of some sort, like you see on some older buildings. Except the ledge came right out of the wall, was about four feet wide, and there was nothing above or below it, except more wall.

Maryann was looking at something in the middle of the room. "Hey, Joey, come over here for a minute. What is this thing?"

Joey walked over to where Maryann was standing. She was looking at something. "That's interesting, it's a sundial."

"A sundial? I guess it goes with this room, but why have a sundial inside a house?"

"Maybe that's the only way people could tell time back when this house was built. That was a long, long time ago."

"Maybe. I guess the sun was the only thing you could count on in those olden days."

"But did you notice anything out of the ordinary about this sundial, Maryann?" Joey's arms were crossed and he had a studious look on his face.

"Other than the fact it's here, in the middle of a Mud House, in a room that's so yellow my eyes hurt? You mean stranger than all that? No, I guess not."

"There's no shadow. The way you told time on a sundial was where the shadow was cast by this pointy thingy right here, I think it's called a shadow caster. And as you can plainly see, there is plenty of sun coming into this room. The shadow caster is in place, but there's no shadow."

"Hmmm, now that you mention it, that does look a little out of place. Maybe if I move the sun dial a little bit." Maryann rotated the sun dial. As she moved the sun dial though, there was still no shadow.

"That is strange, Maryann. With all the light we have in this room, I wonder why there is no shadow. But we don't have a lot of time to think about it now. We're here to find the book from the painting."

Maryann and Joey walked around the room and took everything in. It became apparent rather quickly they would not find a book here. Neither could they leave the way they'd come in. Off in one corner of the room, something caught Joey's eye. He walked over to the corner and stared up at the wall, just over the ledge.

"Maryann, do you see what I'm seeing up there?" Joey asked.

Maryann came over and followed Joey's gaze. She stared and stared. Finally, she said, "You mean the outline on the yellow wall."

"Yes, it is an outline then, I wasn't sure I was actually seeing it. It's kind of shaped like a small door. It's a very faint outline and it blends in so well with all the yellow. But I think it definitely has the look of a door."

"Well, let's go up and see."

"That's a great idea, Maryann," Joey said to his younger charge, "but even if you stood on my shoulders, we wouldn't be able to reach that ledge."

"Who said anything about standing on your shoulders? All you need to do is throw me up there."

"Throw you up there?" Now Joey was a pretty good baseball player and had a good arm, but even he didn't see how he could throw Maryann up there.

"Well, not throw, throw. But more like a gymnastic vault. You get down in a crouch; I'll go across the room and run at you. Here, hold your hands like this. Maryann cupped her hands together to show Joey. There, then I'll hop into your hands and you'll boost me up. It's easy. I can make it. I do stuff like this all the time at Arnie's gymnastics academy."

Joey looked skeptical. Maryann nodded her head hopefully. Joey figured he had nothing to lose.

"OK, if you're sure about this, we can give it a try. On three, OK? One…two…three!"

Maryann began running towards Joey, hopped into his hands and he boosted her up towards the ledge. In what Joey would swear later was slow motion, Maryann did a somersault in midair and stuck the landing on the ledge perfectly. Arms spread out and knees slightly bent. "Piece of cake," Maryann said as she turned around.

Joey was standing below her with his mouth wide open, shaking his head. "Maryann, that was unbelievable. Where did you learn to do that?"

"Like I said, at Arnie's, where else?"

"Maryann, maybe we got ahead of ourselves, but how am I going to get up there? I can't jump that high."

Maryann began walking around the ledge when she suddenly smiled. Here, see if this helps. She kicked something over the ledge.

Joey ran over and saw a pure yellow rope-ladder tumbling over the ledge. "Awesome, Maryann! I'll be right up." Joey scrambled up the rope and Maryann helped him onto the outcropping. Together, they walked over to the faint outline they'd seen from below.

"Maryann, do you hear that?" Joey asked.

"Hear what? I don't hear anything."

"It sounds like, I don't know, like a buzzing sound. Like hundreds of bees. Like a big beehive or something."

"No, I don't hear any bees," Maryann answered. "Are you feeling OK? Let's forget about the bees and see if this door can help us."

Joey began to feel around the outline and gently pushed on the center. The door swung inward. Joey and Roxie stepped inside a small room. The door began to swing shut behind them. Joey made a grab for the door but missed. Joey barely noticed, but the bee sounds stopped when the door closed on them. There was no handle from the inside to help them open the door. "Well, now we're here at least. But exactly where is here?"

"I don't…"

Before Joey could finish his sentence, the floor dropped out from under the two children. They fell onto a slide-like chute and began sliding downward. Down, down, down they slid as they hollered the whole way. Finally, they popped out of the chute onto a large bed of straw. The kids were coughing and getting bits of straw out of their mouths when Joey felt something grab his shoulder.

"Ahhhhh…" Joey yelled.

CHAPTER 9 – All Together Now

"Ahhhh..." Joey was still yelling because somebody grabbed his shoulder after he and Maryann slid down the chute.

"Joey, what's the matter with you?" Billy asked as he took his hand off his brother's shoulder.

"Billy? What are you doing? You scared me almost half to death. Where are we? What is going on?"

"I'm not sure exactly. Roxie and I were climbing out of a trap door that led from the star room to this place just as Erick and Rose were coming out of a tunnel over there." Billy pointed towards a doorway across the room. "We were talking about how we all got here when we heard a bunch of yelling and screaming. We ran over here just as you and Maryann fell into this big pile of straw."

"Wait a minute. Are you saying we all found some sort of secret passageway from the Mud House to this, this...what is this place?"

It looks like some sort of barn or something," Erick replied. "And we're not alone, take a look up there."

Joey looked towards the ceiling and saw hundreds of little eyes peering back at him. Bats! The barn was full of bats. Joey shivered.

Joey and Maryann got up and dusted themselves off. "It does kind of look like a barn... smells like one too, even with all the bats. Remember, you read that off the card in the foyer? The card said a barn was built after the original Mud House. I'll bet this is the barn."

"Joey, did you guys find the book? Because we didn't find one in the moon room," Rose said impatiently.

"No. No Rose, we didn't find a book or anything except the door to the chute that led us here."

"OK. Black belt or no black belt, I'm starting to worry," Erick chimed in.

"Hang on Erick, we'll be fine, you'll see," Roxie said hopefully. A little more worried herself now that her big brother was showing some of his concern.

"Of course we will. No question about that. Let's see if this barn has a door. Every barn has a door," Billy said hopefully.

"We're basically back to where we started. We're all together again and it's probably best that we stick together until we get out of here. Does everyone agree?" Joey asked the group.

They all nodded their heads in the affirmative.

"The thing we have to remember is…"

But Joey never got to finish his sentence because suddenly, all the lights in the barn went out at once.

An evil sounding laugh filled the barn. "Now you've fallen into my trap, my little kiddies. Prepare yourselves."

The Wild Bunch and the Joditz kids were standing in a circle, holding onto each other as they listened to the voice shout at them.

"I am the Great Tater. This is my lair. You have trespassed and for that…you will pay. What do you have to say for yourselves before judgment is passed?"

A large and distorted face appeared against the far wall of the barn. It was out of focus, and looked like a clown with a very bad makeup job. Was that orange hair, or an orange nose? It was very hard to tell.

"T…T…Tater?" Joey ventured.

"The *Great* Tater!" the Great Tater yelled back.

"Uhhhh, Mr. Great Tater, sir…we were just looking for something in the Mud House. We got lost and found ourselves in this place. We're hoping to find what we're looking for and then head back home. We'll get out of your…hair. In fact, maybe…"

"Lost!? How can you be lost when the Great Tater knows exactly where you are?" shouted the Great Tater. Suddenly a great grinding noise was heard across the barn and sparks began to fly across the room.

"Listen you big bozo, just because you know where we are doesn't mean we do!" shouted Rose, reaching down inside herself and finding her defiant spirit. She wasn't going to be bullied by some two-bit clown!

"Who dares yell at the Great Tater?" Tater asked.

"Shhhhhh!" Billy said to Rose. "You don't want to get this Tater guy any angrier with us than he already is!"

"Well, if he's angry, then I'm angry too. We just want to find our book and get home Mr. Tater-head!" Rose shouted.

"Who dares mock the Great Tater?" Tater asked. Now there was a fog drifting across the barn floor, adding to the creepiness of the whole encounter. A few flashes of lightning and sounds like thunder reverberated inside the barn.

Maryann and Billy began to move away from the group towards a sliver of light they saw on the other side of the barn through the darkness. When they reached the sliver of light, they noticed black construction paper covering a window. The lightning, thunder and fog continued to roll through the structure of the barn. The Great Tater continued demanding to know who would dare challenge him.

"Ah, you don't sound so tough, Tater-boy," Roxie said, joining hands with Rose to steel her confidence.

"WHAT!" the Great Tater shouted. "Then you are perilously close to experiencing the full wrath of the Great Tater!" Thunder upon rolling thunder clap filled the barn. The lightning was blinding, sparks were flying. The bats had all left the barn through a hole in the roof. Then suddenly and without warning there was…silence…simply silence.

"Uh oh," was all Joey could say. "I think we're in trouble now."

Joey was right. In a million years, he could not have anticipated what was to come next.

CHAPTER 10 – Unmasked

A few seconds before the noise in the barn stopped, Billy and Maryann had begun to tear at the construction paper to allow more light to flow into the barn. As they tore away at the paper, they could hear the Great Tater yelling at the rest of the kids. The lightning and thunder reached a frenzied pace. Billy ran to the next window but he tripped over something and suddenly…that was when the barn grew completely silent. Billy looked down to discover he had tripped over an electrical cord.

"Oh, now you've done it. You pulled my plug! Just when things were getting good," said a boy with dark curly hair. The boy was coming out from behind an old shower curtain a few feet from where Billy had tripped. The curly haired boy looked to be about Joey's age. He was wearing a long black cape that reminded Billy of a vampire.

"Who…who are you?" a surprised Billy asked from the floor.

"Hi, I'm Shep Tater. My friends call me Shep. You can call me Shep. Here let me help you up." Shep bent down and helped Billy get off of the floor. "There you go. Let's plug that back in, right there." Shep Tater put the plug back into an outlet and all the noise and commotion started up again. He ran behind the shower curtain. In just a couple of seconds, the noise stopped and the lights came

65

up in the barn.

By this time, the rest of the Wild Bunch and the Joditz kids ran over to where Billy had tripped. Billy had a shocked expression on his face. "Uh, guys, I'd like you to meet Shep Tater."

"Are you the Great Tater-head?" Rose asked.

"It's just the Great Tater. No head. Yes, the one and only. I am pleased to make your acquaintance." Shep bowed.

"You mean, you're behind all of this?" Joey asked as he swooped his arm in an arc over his head.

"Yes sir. I am the one and the same. I've been watching you since you came up the driveway earlier today."

"Oh, so you wrote the note we found?" Joey asked.

Shep looked at Joey. "Yes, I wrote the note and locked the doors behind you. I wanted to test my little project and you guys looked like a fine group to walk through it to see if it was any good."

"And what, exactly, is your little project?" asked Maryann.

"Oh. I thought it would have been obvious to you by now. No? OK. You've just been the first visitors to the trial-run of Tater's Terror House! Get it? This is going to be my haunted house for Halloween this year. What do you think?"

"Who, exactly, are you?" asked Joey, picking straw out of his clothes he collected during his fall.

"Like I said before, I'm Shep Tater. I just moved here from Rhode Island with my family. My mom is down at Michael Scott's getting her hair done. We haven't been here very long but she loves that place."

"Hey, my dad goes to Michael Scott's to get his hair cut too!" Rose volunteered.

"I'm going to the middle school next year here in Mansfield. Our house is a bit isolated and I haven't met very many people yet, until you guys, that is. So how did you like my haunted house?"

"Umm…Shep is it? Well Shep, you scared us but good! Your haunted house is going to be a hit if this is only your trial run. My name is Joey Wild. I'm going to be at the Qualters Middle School next year too. This is my brother Billy, and my sister Rose. These guys are Erick, Maryann and Roxie Joditz. We live up the road from here. We were on our way to Erick's fort when we got lost. Eventually, we found our way to the Mud House. That's when we saw the painting and began looking for the book."

"The painting? Oh, you mean the painting in the foyer? The painting with all those people in it? I don't remember seeing a book in that painting though, only people."

"Shep, we saw that painting change several times, as unbelievable as that sounds. We think the people in the painting were sending us a message. They want us to find the book. We don't know why. Do you have any idea what that's all about?"

"Hmmmm…a book you say? Well in my note to you I…"

"How did you get this stuff set up so quickly?" Billy interrupted Shep.

"Oh, you mean the barn?" Shep asked.

"Yeah, that and the secret passages to the barn," Erick chimed in.

"Well, most of the stuff in the barn I brought with me from Rhode Island. It's just a stereo with a microphone, some stuff from my dad's machine shop and some dry ice. The shower curtain is my favorite. It wasn't all that hard really. Since there was no school, I just had time to work on it during the day."

"That makes sense," Maryann said. "But what about the secret passage ways and weird rooms?"

"Now that's a different story. That's the decor the house came with. The previous owners had a, let's call it unique, touch for decorating. We even found evidence of an old bee house up on the second floor."

67

Joey thought back to the buzzing he heard in the honey colored room he and Maryann found.

"As for the passage ways, all I know is what I heard from our realtor, Jake Frost."

"Jake Frost?" Roxie inquired.

"Yeah, Jake Frost, he's a big time realtor around here," Shep said.

"And what exactly did Jake Frost say?" Joey asked.

"Apparently, this house is very close to an old home in East Mansfield that was part of the Underground Railroad network before the Civil War. That home is down by the East Mansfield Common across Route 106 and past Slate's Farm. Oftentimes in homes along the route, tunnels and passageways lead from the main house to someplace else. Sort of like an escape route. There's no direct evidence the Mud House was part of the network, but I like to think it could have been. The Stearns family was apparently very supportive of the Union."

"Wow, that's pretty cool. I never knew that," Joey said, somewhat amazed that his little town of Mansfield could have had stops on the Underground Railroad system. "But you were getting ready to say something about the book, before Billy interrupted you. Do you have any ideas?"

Shep looked at Joey. Then he looked at everyone in the group. "You know, I think there is something I have to show you. I mentioned it in the note I left on the front door. I didn't realize it then, but I think it might be connected. But if I show it to you, you can't tell anybody about it. It goes beyond explanation. Can you guys keep a secret?"

The Wild Bunch and Joditz kids nodded. What were they getting themselves into?

If they only knew, maybe they would have made a different decision.

CHAPTER 11 – Tree House Tricks

"Great, follow me everyone!" And with that Shep began running away from the kids towards the back yard at full speed.

"Hey Shep, wait up!" yelled Joey as he and the others ran after their new friend. "Where are you going?"

Shep turned and beckoned them to follow him. "You'll see, it's right down here."

"What's right down here?" a curious Rose wondered.

Shep ran between the Mud House and the barn into his backyard. He ran past the chicken coop (which had a rooster or two in residence) and down the backyard's big hill. He continued past a stand of bamboo you would have never expected to see in these woods, but there it was. All of a sudden Shep stopped and held up his hand for everyone to do the same, just like the crossing guards did over at the Robinson when school was in session. The Wild Bunch and Joditz kids caught up. They were out of breath and breathing hard. Rose and Roxie were bent over, hands on their knees, trying to catch their breath.

"Here we are. What do you think?" an excited Shep asked.

Everyone just looked around. All they could see was woods, the Mud House at the top of the hill and the backyard. There was a gargoyle standing guard in front of a big pine tree, but they couldn't see anything else. Each child exchanged bewildered looks amongst themselves.

Erick spoke up first, "Hey Shep, the race was fun and all, but I don't see anything. Cool or not cool, I don't get it."

Shep smiled. "It's all about perspective, Erick. Sometimes, you have to change your view on the world to see what others see. You know? Expect the unexpected."

"Like that painting!" Rose exclaimed.

Shep replied, "That painting again. Well, if it changes like you say it does, then yes, that could be an example of changing perspective."

"OK, Shep, I hear what you're saying, but I still don't see what you want us to see," Erick pointed out.

"That's because you're not really *seeing* it."

"I know, I just said that."

Shep smiled again, a bigger smile this time. Then, slowly, he pointed towards the sky.

At first, the kids looked at each other. They shook their heads. Then, their gaze shifted upwards. One by one, their eyes got big and their mouths dropped open.

"That's sick!" Joey exclaimed.

"Makes my fort look like a tiny log creation gone bad," Erick said almost to himself.

"I told you it was cool," replied a nodding Shep.

The kids were staring at a huge tree house. This was no ordinary tree house. This one had at least two floors and a peaked roof. There was a ladder heading up to the middle of the tree house and a single solitary pole to slide down for a fast exit. It spanned across two or three trees in the backyard. It looked like a small house had dropped from the sky and landed in these trees. None of them had ever seen anything quite like it before.

"Can we climb up and go inside?" an exuberant Billy

pleaded.

"Yeah, there's something I want to show you up there. Be careful climbing up though, it doesn't look that high, but it can be tricky."

You didn't have to tell these kids twice! One by one, they ran to the base of the biggest tree and climbed up the wooden ladder nailed right into the tree itself. The ladder led to the middle of the tree house where a trap door led into a large main room.

There was enough room for everyone to comfortably sit in a circle. Shep was the last to climb up and take his place in the circle. As the kids looked around the room, they saw chairs, boxes that could be used as tables, some comic books and another ladder going up to the second level of the tree house.

"What do you think?" he asked.

"This is awesome," Roxie replied. "How did you build this?"

"I didn't. It was here when we moved in. You can see for quite a distance, all around Mansfield, from right here. At night, I can even hear the train zooming through Mansfield's train station. And that's over three miles away!"

Joey jumped in, "I think you'll be able to see the fireworks they shoot off during the Pat's games. The football season begins in Foxboro in just a couple of months. I think they are going to win the Super Bowl again this year. The coach is putting together a great team. Their first round draft choice is going to be awesome someday, and so are all the other guys they drafted this year. This is an awesome view!"

"What's upstairs?" Billy asked.

"It's a room like this one, except a little bit smaller. Come on, I'll show you. Besides, what I really want you to see is up there too." And with that, Shep began to scramble up a second, smaller ladder to the second level.

Joey and Billy just looked at each other. It was Billy who

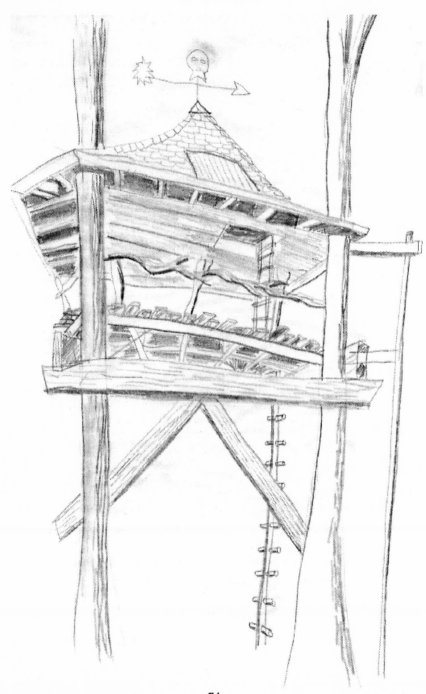

said, "There's *more* he wants us to see? How do you top this?"

"I don't know, Billy. But let's get up there and find out!"

Joey and Billy were the last to make it up to the second level of the tree house. The room was a little bit smaller, but everyone was able to sit comfortably and face one another. A couple of windows overlooked the Mud House and more of Mansfield was visible from here too. Another small table was in one corner of the room. There was an old fashioned telephone on the desk.

Shep began talking, "I found this tree house by accident. Jake Frost didn't say a word about it to my parents. I don't think he knew it was even here. I haven't told my parents about my little discovery yet."

"Why not?" Roxie asked.

"Good question, Roxie. The answer to that is what I want to show you. It's the reason I've kept this to myself. I'm not quite sure what to make of my latest discovery. But you said something in the barn that made me think you might know more about this than me."

"What do you want to show us, Shep? What discovery?" Rose asked the very question Joey and Billy had wondered about earlier.

Shep smiled again. He nodded his head and stood up. Then he walked slowly over to the lone table in the room and opened a drawer. From the drawer he took something out. Shep closed the drawer and returned to the circle with the object.

Shep was holding what looked like a large black book. But it was very old and dusty looking.

"This is what I found," Shep said, holding the book up for everyone to see. "It's old. Notice these numbers here? I think it's a date. It says 1675. If this book was made in 1675, that makes it over 325 years old!"

The Wild Bunch and the Joditz kids just stared. Then they

looked at one another. They couldn't believe their eyes. But it was true.

"Shep," Joey said, "That's the book we saw in the painting. That must be the book we've been looking for!" Joey was very excited. "But I wonder what the book has to do with the Mud House."

Shep shook his head. "This is no ordinary book. I'm not sure it's what you are looking for, but I need to show you something else."

Shep opened the book and held it up for everyone to see. It was not a real book at all. You couldn't get this book from the Mansfield Public Library. It was a fake book. There were no real pages inside. There was just a hollow space where the pages should have been. No, not even one page. But there was something else. Something that didn't make any sense at all to any of the kids in the treehouse. Shep was smiling.

At that moment, somebody in the tree house screamed!

CHAPTER 12 – Which Way Do We Go?

"Maryann, stop screaming!" Roxie exclaimed as she tried to calm her little sister.

"But there is something crawling on me. It feels like a bug. Or maybe a spider. Get it off me!"

"Maryann, there's nothing crawling on you. It's just a big leaf that fell through the ceiling, that's all. See, it fell right there on your leg." Roxie was holding up the leaf for Maryann to inspect.

"Oh. Sorry about that," an embarrassed Maryann said to the group. "I thought it was a bug…or a spider."

Everyone else breathed a big sigh of relief. Shep was still holding open the fake book for everyone to see. He was still smiling. Inside there was a small, round object.

"What is that, Shep?" Billy asked.

"I think it's a compass. But look closely. There's something wrong with this compass?"

"What's a compass?" Rose asked.

Joey looked at his little sister. They probably hadn't got to studying compasses yet at the Robinson school. "A compass is used to figure out what direction you're going or the direction you would like to go."

"Why do you need a compass?" Maryann piped in. "Don't you always know the direction you're going? Like, I'm going to school. Or I'm going to the store. Why would I need a compass?"

Joey replied, "Sometimes, you don't know exactly where you're going. You might only know a distance or a direction. A compass can be used with a map or landmarks to help you find your way from one point to another. It helps you to travel in the right direction from different points on a map."

"Hey," Erick said, "Maybe we can use the compass to help us get back home."

"Good idea, Erick!" Maryann said, proud of her big brother's suggestion and hoping they would be home soon.

"Erick, remember, I know how to get home. So don't worry about that. I don't think we'll need a compass to find our way home. I'm wondering what this compass has to do with the book and with the Mud House."

"Normally, I'd agree with you, Erick," Shep said. "But look closely at this compass. Do you see what I see?"

"No, not really. Can you take it out of the book?" Erick asked.

"Sure," Shep replied. He took the compass out of the book and handed it to Erick. "Do you see that? The needle is spinning. It's out of control. It is supposed to point North, but it doesn't. It's just spinning around and around."

"You're right," Erick said, handing the compass to Roxie.

"Yep. The needle is spinning. Like a top. What's wrong with it?" Roxie passed the compass along in the circle.

"I don't know. I found the book in the Mud House and brought it out to the tree house to read. Then I found the compass inside. It's been spinning ever since I found it. It won't stop."

Rose was examining the compass. She just shook her head and passed it to Billy. He did the same. The compass was making its way around the circle of friends.

"That's too bad," Erick said. "But Shep, you said you found

the book *inside* of the Mud House?"

"Yes, that's right. I found it under the stairs behind some old boxes the previous owners left behind. It was shortly after we moved in."

"How close were those stairs to that old painting?" Erick asked.

"Well, now that I think about it, the painting is on the other side of the same wall as the stairs."

"Hmmm…I wonder…" Erick thought out loud.

Finally, the compass made its way to Joey. He took the compass and looked at it for a second. He looked at everyone in the group. Then he looked back down at the compass and shook it again. He had a worried look on his face.

"Joey, what's wrong?" Rose asked.

"Well, I hate to tell you guys this," Joey hesitated a second more. "But I think I broke the compass."

Erick looked at Joey. Shep walked over to where Joey was sitting. He took the compass from Joey and looked at it. "What do you mean you broke it?" Shep asked.

"I don't know. I just think I broke it or something."

By this time, Erick had made his way over to where Shep was standing. He looked over Shep's shoulder and saw the spinning needle of the compass, just like before. "Hey Shep, let me see the compass again for a second."

Shep handed the compass to Erick. Erick looked at it. It was the same. No change. He looked at the compass for a second more, then he looked at Joey. "Joey, here, take the compass again." Erick handed the compass back to Joey.

"Are you sure? I didn't mean to break it. I'm sorry Shep," Joey said, feeling pretty bad about breaking the compass. He took the compass from Erick. Erick stood over Joey's shoulder as he held onto it.

"See, it's broken," Joey said. "I didn't mean to break it."

Erick started laughing.

Joey looked up at Erick and asked, "What's so funny?"

Erick stopped laughing and said, "I'm sorry Joey. I'm not laughing at you."

"Then what are you laughing at?"

"It's what Shep has been saying all along. Perspective. I'm laughing at our perspective! The riddle was right!"

"I don't get it," Billy said. "You're talking in circles Erick. What gives?"

"OK. OK. Sorry. Joey, why do you think you broke the compass?" Erick asked.

"Well, you guys said the needle was spinning around and around, right?"

Erick nodded his head and smiled. "Keep going, Joey."

"But when I got the compass, the needle stopped spinning. I broke it! I'm sorry!"

"Let me see that, Joey."

Joey handed the compass to Shep.

Shep looked at the compass. No, it was the same. The needle was spinning, out of control. He handed it back to Joey. Joey took the compass, confusion on his face. Looking over Joey's shoulder, Shep saw what Erick had just seen. Shep's jaw dropped open and then he smiled.

"What? What is it?" Maryann asked.

"Joey didn't break the compass. He fixed it!" Shep exclaimed. "Maybe fix it isn't quite right, because the needle still spins whenever anybody *but* Joey is holding onto it." Shep looked over at Erick, who nodded his agreement.

"What?" Roxie said, jumping up from her place in the circle and coming over to stand behind Joey. Sure enough, the compass was at a dead stop. The needle was pointing in one direction.

"Wait a minute," Joey said as the realization hit him. "If this is true, then maybe the compass is telling us where we need to go next! But where exactly, is that?"

The kids all jumped up and gathered around Joey. He looked at the kids and stood up. He walked over to one of the windows in the tree house. The needle was still pointing in one direction. He looked down at the needle. He looked out the window. Then back to the needle. Finally he turned around to face the others.

"Joey, what's it pointing to? Where do we need to go?" Roxie asked.

Joey turned back around and pointed out of the window. "Over there. We have to take the book back home."

"Home?" Rose asked. "Why do we need to take the book back to Colonial Drive?"

"Not our home, Rose. We need to take the book to the book's home. We have to go back into the Mud House."

They sure did.

CHAPTER 13 – Zipping Along

"The Mud House?" Erick asked. "Do we have to? That place gives me the creeps."

"Erick, I don't think we have any choice, do you?" Joey replied. "Think back to the painting. The way it changed each time somebody else held the book. When the book finally disappeared, everybody in the painting was unhappy. Somehow, the Mud House needs this book. It's not happy when the book isn't *home*. I think maybe that is what the people in the painting were trying to tell us."

"Joey, you may be on to something," Shep offered. "I never really thought about this before now, but shortly after I found the book and brought it here to the tree house, the house didn't *feel* right. Clocks ran backwards, the TV wouldn't work right, doors would lock all by themselves, the phone wouldn't work and the air conditioner didn't cool anymore. My mom and dad thought they were going crazy. We didn't understand why everything in the house began breaking all of a sudden. And it all started after I took the book away from the Mud House."

"I think we should take the book back to the Mud House, Joey, don't you?" Maryann asked.

"I think you're right, Maryann," Joey replied.

"Let's climb down and get going then," Billy said.

"Climb? You want to climb down, Billy? But that's *so* slow," a grinning Shep said. "Let me show you the last surprise this old tree house has to offer. Come over here with me." Shep made his way to one corner of the tree house and opened a small door. The kids gathered around the small opening. "That looks like a long way down," Joey said.

"Oh it is a long way down. And climbing down isn't as easy as climbing up. But whoever built this tree house thought of everything. Take a look at this." Shep stood out of the way and let the others get a good look. Outside of the small door was a three foot plank that led from the tree house to a small platform and some strange looking contraption.

"What's that?" Roxie asked.

Shep answered her, "It's called a zip line. All you have to do is walk across the plank and grab onto the handle and jump off of the platform. Then you'll slide down into the backyard as quick as a bunny."

"Are you sure, Shep?" Rose inquired.

"You bet. I'll go first. But if anyone is scared, feel free to use the fireman's pole over there. Does anyone want to use the pole?"

Everyone shook their head no. They all wanted to give the zip line a try.

"Joey, you should zip down last to make sure everyone gets to the ground without any problems."

Joey nodded.

"OK, here I go!" And with that, Shep carefully walked the plank, grabbed the handle and flung himself off of the platform. Sure enough, he zipped down into the trees and landed somewhere in the back yard.

One by one, each of the kids took their turn on the zip line until Joey brought up the rear, holding onto the book with the compass inside.

"That was cool! Can we do it again?" Billy asked.

It was Erick who said, "Billy, the zip line was a ton of fun, but we have to return the book and get home, remember?"

"You're right, Erick. How hard is it going to be to return this book?" Joey asked while holding up the book for all to see. "It's going to be a piece of cake."

The kids began running up the hill back towards the Mud House. Everyone was laughing and having a good time.

As it turns out, Joey was wrong. Reuniting the book with the Mud House was going to be anything but a piece of cake.

CHAPTER 14 – Amazing

As the kids stopped to catch their breath at the rear of the Mud House, Shep made his way to the front of the group. He opened the screen door and turned the door knob. It didn't budge. He looked back at the group. They looked back at him. He turned and tried the knob again. This time, the door opened. "Whew, I thought we were going to be locked out. Come on in."

The Wild Bunch and the Joditz kids filed into the Mud House kitchen and gathered around the table. Joey put the book on the kitchen table. Like most of the other rooms in the house, the kitchen was pie shaped.

"OK, let's put this book back where you found it Shep, what do you say?" Joey asked.

"Sure thing. Follow me." Shep led the group out of the kitchen into a small ante room near what looked to be the middle of the house. It was hard to tell with the shape of the house exactly where you were at any given time. "I found the book inside of this room in a small drawer behind some abandoned boxes. The stairs heading to the second floor are on the other side of the wall. That's where the foyer is too. You remember the foyer, right?"

The kids nodded. Billy thought back to the odd painting hanging on the other side of the wall.

"Hand me the book, Joey," Shep said.

Joey handed the book to Shep. The ante room was too small for everyone.

"OK, let me move these boxes…"

The kids could hear Shep moving boxes around the floor of the ante room. After a moment or two, there was silence. The silence was followed by the sound of boxes being shuffled around again. Shep reappeared.

"Great," Joey said. "Let's get going everyone."

"Ah, Joey?"

"Yeah, Shep? What's up?" Joey asked.

"We've got a problem."

"What kind of problem, Shep?"

"The drawer is missing. It's not there. I have no place to put the book." Shep said as he showed everyone he still had the book.

The group of kids groaned.

"What do you mean the drawer is gone, Shep?" Joey asked.

"Just like I said, Joey. It's gone. There's nothing there but walls and boxes. I can't explain it. It was there before. Now it's not."

"OK, let's think about this for a second. Can I see the book?"

Shep handed Joey the book.

Joey opened the book. There was the compass. Its hand spinning wildly. Out of control. Joey sighed. "I don't believe this. What's wrong?" The book is back in the house."

"Maybe it's not really where it's supposed to be," Rose offered.

Joey looked at Rose and said nothing. Sometimes, she made more sense with simple statements like that than any of them did when they talked all the time. "You might be right, Rose."

Rose smiled.

Joey reached for the compass and removed it from the book. As he did so, the hand on the compass began to slow down, until finally, it stopped.

"What do we do now, Joey?" Billy asked.

"We go where the compass tells us to go. We move in the direction it's pointing. Follow me."

Joey began to walk slowly out of the ante room. He would take a few steps in one direction, watch the needle and adjust his course as he went along. The kids followed along behind Joey. He walked out of the ante room to a door. The needle urged him to continue straight through the door. He opened the door and walked through it.

Joey and the group found themselves in the star room.

"Hey, I know this place!" Billy said. "It's our star room, Roxie."

Roxie nodded.

Joey continued to check his compass bearing and walked across the room. Billy wondered how they could have missed this door the first time they were in the room. You couldn't even see it from inside the room. Billy thought that this Stearns fellow must have been a genius by the way he built this house with all its secrets.

Joey kept walking across the room to the door Billy and Roxie had come through the first time. Joey tried the door. It was still locked. "I guess this is the end of the line, then. The door is locked. We'll never solve this mystery." Joey said sadly.

"Don't give up so fast, Joey," Shep said. "Don't forget, I have this." He pulled the skeleton key out of his pocket and walked up to the door. He inserted the key and turned. A loud click as the lock tumbled open. Shep turned the doorknob and the door swung open. "There you go!"

"Thanks, Shep. The needle indicates we should keep going this way." Joey walked through the door. The others followed him.

The group found themselves back in the foyer. Joey looked down at his compass and he made a left turn. Joey continued to walk forward. Then he stopped and looked up. He was staring up at the painting. Joey looked around. He began walking away from the painting. The compass began spinning wildly the further away he got from the painting. Joey stopped and began walking towards the painting again. The needle slowed and pointed straight at the painting again. Joey was perplexed.

"Ahh, Joey?" Erick asked.

"Yeah, Erick, hang on, I'm trying to figure this out," Joey replied.

"I know, Joey. I think I have an idea."

"What is it?" Joey asked, turning towards Erick.

Erick didn't say anything else, he simply pointed towards the painting. Joey turned around and looked up at the picture.

Everyone in the painting was standing up now. It looked like they were pointing right at Joey. He felt the hair on the back of his neck stand on end. "Why are they pointing at me?" Joey asked.

"Joey, I don't think they are pointing at you. I think they are pointing down here, towards the bottom of the frame," Maryann said. She was on level with the bottom of the frame and to her, it looked like the people in the painting were pointing there.

"What is that?" Shep asked as he stepped closer to where Maryann was standing. He peered closely for a minute and then smiled. "It's the drawer! It's on this side of the wall now. I don't know how, but there it is!" Shep opened the drawer.

Joey handed the book to Shep.

Shep took the book and put it inside of the open drawer. Once the drawer was completely closed, he peered up at the painting, and smiled. Everyone in the painting was again seated and smiling. This time, the woman in the middle of the painting was holding the book. She had the biggest smile on her face. "I think the book is finally back where it's supposed to be," Shep said.

Just as Shep looked up at the painting, the moon, and the sun doors unlocked and swung open. Rose ran into the moon room and looked around. She saw the clock Erick and her had spied earlier and ran over to it. It was running forward now, not backwards.

Roxie ducked into the star room and peered into the telescope. No book this time. All she could see was a close up of whatever in the room she pointed the telescope towards.

At the same time, Joey ran up the stairs to the sun room. He walked over to the sun dial and saw…a shadow. The sun dial was working perfectly too.

All of the kids gathered back together in the foyer. The house air conditioner had kicked on and the room temperature was dropping. Somewhere in the house, a TV was blaring. And everyone was smiling.

"That was something else!" Shep said. "The book fixed our house. It's like the Mud House is happy again. And all because of the book in this drawer right…" Shep stopped in mid sentence. He peered closely at the spot where the drawer *should* have been. But it wasn't there. The drawer and the book inside of it were both gone. But the people in the painting were still smiling.

"Shep, I guess this is your official welcome to Mansfield. I can't explain everything that went on here today, but this summer just gets more interesting every time we leave our house," Joey said.

"Yeah, I'm starting to see what you mean," Shep replied, shaking his head.

"Hey guys, we have to get going. We don't want to be late for the Joditz cookout," Joey reminded the group.

The Wild Bunch and the Joditz kids made their way to the front door. "I'm not sure I can take much more adventure this summer. I just want to relax and enjoy doing nothing all day. Shep it was good meeting you. You'll have to come up and visit us when you're taking a break from your haunted house, OK?" Joey said with a smile.

"Sure thing, Joey. I'm glad to have friends like you all. Thanks for everything. My parents are going to be so happy when they get home and see that our new home is back to normal. I can't thank you all enough. Bye." Shep was waving to the Wild Bunch and Joditz kids.

Everyone was relaxed and very happy as they made their way down the driveway. They turned and gave Shep a last wave before setting off in earnest to the Joditz cookout. As the Wild Bunch and Joditz kids headed up Stearns Avenue towards the fun they knew was just around the corner, they looked forward to a calm remainder of the summer. What the Wild Bunch didn't know, of course, was that the rest of their summer vacation was going to be anything but calm. In fact, their unforgettable summer was about to get even MORE unforgettable!

THE END

Kids, you don't want to miss the next Wild Bunch Adventure! Join Joey, Billy and Rose and all their friends as they find themselves in another exciting adventure during the most unforgettable summer of their lives. They never thought there was so much going on in the little town of Mansfield. Did you? You can keep up with the Wild Bunch at *www.the-wild-bunch.com.*

And if you missed the Wild Bunch in *The Mystery of the Golden Skate*, it's not too late to get your copy! Be sure to pick up the first Wild Bunch Adventure online or just ask for it at your favorite local bookstore.

Meet The Mud House Characters

Joey Wild is eleven years old and loves to play all sports. But his favorite sport is baseball and his favorite positions are third base and pitcher. Joey was born in Texas and moved to Mansfield when he was very young. He's looking forward to Middle School, but not riding the bus at 7:00 in the morning. As the oldest Wild child, Joey is counted on by his brother and sister to keep a level head and keep them out of jams.

Billy Wild is nine years old and loves to play baseball and go swimming. He enjoys reading and is good at math and science. Billy just finished the third grade where his teacher challenged the class to push beyond their comfort zones and reach new, stupendous heights. He thinks of himself as a secret agent, and enjoys solving mysteries and puzzles using his active imagination and keen sense of humor.

Rose Wild is the youngest of the Wild Bunch at seven, but don't under estimate her. Having two older brothers always keeps her on her toes (which helps her during gymnastics classes too).

After this exciting summer, Rose will enter the first grade, which is OK with her because she loves school and learning new things. Always the voice of reason and clarity, you can count on Rose for a perspective her brothers may not have considered.

Erick Joditz is ten years old and already a karate black belt. Known around the neighborhood as a sports loving guy, Erick is always up for a game of baseball, basketball or football. Erick loves to swim in his pool when he's not helping his mom and dad around the house.

Roxie Joditz is eight years old and is looking forward to entering the third grade. She's eager to learn, and also likes to draw, just like her mom. Roxie loves to ride her bike as fast as she can all around her neighborhood. Idolizing her big brother, she'll do anything for him as they roam the neighborhood looking for fun.

Maryann Joditz is six years old and is a standout gymnast. You can find her during the summer doing round offs up and down her driveway, almost all day long. Maryann has a keen sense of humor and being the youngest, doesn't take any grief from her older siblings.

Shep Tater is eleven years old and lives in the Mud House. Shep and his family just moved to town but he's looking forward to Middle School. Shep loves acting and the arts and his spook house promises to be one of the best around.

Coach Joditz is employed by Calamity Demolition Services and lives in the Wild's neighborhood. Active as a Little League coach, Joditz can be found at the Otis Street Fields during baseball season where he helps the kids hone their skills. If he's not there, look for him as he drives a large red dump truck from job to job around town.

Mrs. Joditz is an artist and avid volleyball player. Belonging to at least three competitive leagues at any one time certainly prepares her for anything her three children might throw at her. If she's not at home or at the volleyball courts, see if you can spot her around town on her Harley motorcycle.

Mrs. Wild is the mother of The Wild Bunch who keeps the kids on the move and out of trouble. She enjoys gardening, a clean house and collects baskets by the dozens. Her biggest challenge is finding 'quiet' time in a house full of Wilds. It doesn't happen often, but when it does, Mrs. Wild likes to read or work in her garden.

Hey Kids!
Don't Dare Miss:

The Wild Bunch
in

The Sawyer Diamonds Mystery

The Special Sneak Preview starts on the next page!

CHAPTER 1 – Otis Street's Field of Dreams

"Strrrrriiiike One!" shouted the home plate umpire on field five as he pointed his right index finger towards the first base dugout. "The count is three balls and one strike." He held up three fingers on his left hand and one finger on his right hand so the count could be verified by both benches.

The Mansfield Hockomock league baseball team catcher, John Shoto, tossed the ball back to the pitcher's mound.

Joey Wild caught the ball, took off his glove and began rubbing down the baseball. He looked around the baseball diamond and didn't like what he saw. There was some good news and there was some bad news as he surveyed the field.

Mansfield was beating arch rival Norton 3-2. It was the last inning of the Hock championship game. That was the good news. The bad news was that the bases were loaded. There were two outs and Norton was on the verge of pushing across runs.

Joey had been brought into the game to pitch to this Norton batter and, more importantly, to get him out. Joey was facing their clean up hitter. A guy named Screemshaw.

Mansfield starting pitcher Jimmy Rollins had done a great job by allowing only two Norton runs over the first four innings. Jimmy was relieved by Nelson Jenks to start the fifth inning. Nelson pitched brilliantly for one and two-thirds of an inning. There were two outs now, but Norton had managed to load the bases on Nelson.

Joey had a feeling manager Mitch Winkler would call him

over from his first base position to help get Nelson, and the team, out of this late inning jam. Joey loved to pitch in these situations. He never looked nervous or got rattled when he was on the mound. The mound felt like home to him. Joey was comfortable standing on the field five mound. He felt relaxed and in control. Joey knew if he walked this Norton batter in, the game would be tied. The game's momentum would swing Norton's way. Things like that happened sometimes in baseball. One second you're on top of the world, the next second, you're looking for a hole to jump into.

Coach Nadol and coach Cantana were urging Joey on from the home dugout on the third base side of the field. "C'mon Joey, you can get this guy. Throw him strikes at the knees! He can't catch up to your fast ball. Make him be a hitter! Let your fielders do the work."

The infield was playing at normal depth with two outs and the lead. They were poised to get the third out at the easiest base.

Having had a well deserved rest after Nelson relieved him earlier, Jimmy jumped off the bench and took over at first base when Winkler called Joey over to pitch. Jimmy was staring down at the batter, waiting for the pitch. Chuck Jennings was at second base, slapping his glove and eager to make a play. Short stop Craig McRowan was down and ready; his glove already resting lightly on the ground, anticipating the ground ball. Almost nothing got by Craig when the ball was hit in his direction at short stop.

Joey saw that Mick Cantana was playing the line at third. Mick was guarding the line, just like he was supposed to be doing. Joey knew these guys wouldn't let anything get by them. He pulled his glove back onto his left hand. The coaches were right, these guys were ready.

Joey looked in to get the sign from John. John called for the fast ball, outside corner. Joey nodded his agreement and began his deliberate and distinctive wind up. He threw the ball hard, keeping in mind that his goal was to hit John's glove, no matter where John put it. The ball sizzled towards the Norton batter and he swung his bat. It was a late swing, but Screemshaw still got a piece of the baseball. The ball sailed towards the outfield and began tailing back towards the first base line…the Norton runner on third was already two thirds of the way home, having left on contact with the ball. Everybody in the field was moving; they all had places they had to be to help make a play. This was a well coached team.

Right fielder Brad Winkler got a great jump on the ball as it left the bat. He was tracking it down in the outfield. He was moving fast…but not fast enough to keep up with the tailing orb. The ball landed with a thud.

All of the Mansfield fans sitting on the packed third base bleachers were standing up, holding their collective breath. The home plate umpire, running next to the first base line to get a better view of the play suddenly stopped, threw his hands up and yelled… "Foul ball!" The ball landed in foul territory by two feet. A diving Brad landed two and a half feet away, just missing the catch for what would have been the third out. A long strike two. But strike two it was.

Whew, Joey thought to himself, *that was close. Too close.* Brad retrieved the foul ball and threw it to Joey on the pitcher's mound. Joey rubbed up the ball again for a second. Ready. Both feet on the rubber, he looked in for the sign. John flashed him the fast ball sign again. Joey shook him off. John flashed him the fast ball sign again. Again, Joey shook him off. John turned to the umpire and asked for time out. "Time!" yelled the ump.

John trotted to the mound. Jimmy and Craig joined their pitcher and catcher for the conference. "Joey, why don't you want to throw him your fast ball?" John asked.

"He was too close on that last pitch. I want to try and change speeds on him. I want to see if I can mess up his timing.

You know he's looking for a fast ball with a full count on him. I want to fool him," Joey reasoned.

"OK, Joey, go ahead, but it has to be a strike. We can't afford to walk this guy," Craig offered.

"You're right, Craig. I can't walk him. John, this is going to be right down the middle, but I'm throwing my change up," Joey was determined.

"I hope you know what you're doing, Joey." John looked into the dugout at manager Winkler. John had a worried look on his face and shook his head slightly.

"Trust me," Joey said. "We'll get this guy. Let's go play baseball, boys."

Jimmy, Craig and John went back to their positions. Joey brought the glove up to just under his eyes and stared in at the batter. He wasn't nervous at all. He knew he would get this guy. John set up with his glove in the middle of the plate, waist high.

Changing the grip on the ball in his glove for the change up, Joey began his wind up. When he let go of the ball, his motion looked exactly the same to the Norton batter.

The Norton batter's eyes got wide. He read the arm speed and throwing motion and thought to himself, *It's another fat old fast ball and it's coming right down the middle!*

The Norton batter loaded up and swung as hard as he could. The only problem was that Joey's *OK-changeup* grip had slowed the speed of the ball down by about 15 miles an hour from the previous fast ball. The batter realized half way through his swing that the ball wasn't anywhere close to the plate yet! It wasn't the fast ball! He tried to adjust his swing in mid-motion. It didn't work. Screemshaw ended up way off balance. His swing was way in front of the ball, much too early. His mighty swing turned into nothing more than a weak wave at the baseball. A wave that connected with only the thin air around it.

"Strike three! You're out!" yelled the umpire.

The Mansfield fans let out a roar! Outfielders Donny Everson and Stan Nadol threw their gloves into the air and began running towards the infield. Brad from right field was almost there too. They were met from the dugout by the coaches and outfielder Kyle Jones, third baseman Timmy Brinkly, and Nelson, whose arm was already wrapped in an ice pack. There was a huge celebration on the mound. And somewhere in the middle of all that joy was an elated Joey Wild.

They had done it! By beating Norton, the Mansfield Hock team would move on to play in a national tournament in Cooperstown later in the month. They were all very happy. They began to pick themselves up off the ground and get into line to shake the Norton players' hands. After the hand shakes, they ran around the bases and headed out to left field for the traditional post-game meeting.

"Great, Missy," Rose Wild said from behind the right field foul pole. Rose was being sarcastic. "More baseball. I can't wait," she said rolling her eyes at her best friend, Missy Tebold.

"Why can't they ever lose? It's just not fair. I feel like we've been out here every day for the whole, entire summer. Baseball, baseball and, how about some more baseball!"

"It's not so bad, Rose. At least we can get another slushy at the snack shack while they are celebrating over there." Missy replied.

"You're right, Missy. That's looking on the bright side. This time it's my treat. Let's go." Rose and Missy turned around and trotted over to stand in line for their favorite Otis Street treat.

Behind the left field fence, Billy Wild and his buddy, Rick Malloy were watching the celebration on field five. Rick was the same age as Billy, but that's about where all the similarities ended.

Rick was about a foot taller than Billy and had a generous crop of red hair that danced on his head. "What's the big deal, Rick? It's just a baseball game for crying out loud."

"Yeah, but weren't you that happy when your Hock team won the Mansfield and Franklin invitational tournaments earlier this year?" reasoned Rick.

Billy thought for a second and then nodded. "You're right, Rick. I was happy. I guess I'm happy for Joey too…but don't you ever tell him I said that."

"Your secret is safe with me, Billy. I won't tell a soul. Hey, what's up with Mark?" Rick was pointing towards the field five scoreboard. Somebody was yelling and waving their arms while running towards Rick and Billy's position between field five and field six.

That somebody was Mark Herman. Mark was Joey's friend from the neighborhood and lived down the street from both Rick and the Wilds. Mark was a little taller than Joey, but their birthdays were just days apart in August. Mark was an easy going guy who got along with everyone in the neighborhood.

Mark had come to watch Joey's big game and lend him moral support. That's the kind of guy Mark was. Joey, Billy, Mark and Rick could be found almost every summer day playing wiffle ball in the Wild's back yard. Missy and Rose's job during the wiffle ball tournaments was to collect all foul balls that ended up in the Wild's pool or under the deck.

But Mark wasn't excited about wiffle ball, not at this moment anyway.

"Guys, guys! You're not going to believe this." Mark was out of breath from running all this way.

"Hold on, Mark," Billy was holding up his hands. "Catch your breath for a second. What's up? We're all happy Mansfield won the game and all, but it's not that exciting, I mean…"

"No, no, Billy. This has nothing to do with the game. It has to do with something else. Something I can't even begin to explain. It's baseball…not…so many…diamonds…playing. It's just unbelievable!"

For a split second, Billy got an all too familiar eerie feeling. He thought to himself, *Here we go again. First the Golden Skate. Then the Mud House. Now what?? What else could this summer possibly have in store for the Wild Bunch?*

"What are you talking about, Mark," Billy was almost scared to hear his answer. "Of course there are diamonds. This is Otis Street. Seven baseball diamonds," Billy's arm was sweeping in an arc before all of the fields, helping to make his point. "A great complex to be sure. The envy of the Hockomock league. We've played on all of these fields at one time or another, right?"

Rose and Missy had wandered over from the snack shack, blue and red slushy juice covering their lips and tongues. They were listening in on the boys' conversation.

Mark glanced at the girls. He was shaking his head. Billy didn't understand. Mark dug into his right pocket for a minute. He pulled his hand out of his pocket, clutching something in his closed fist. He put his hand out, fist still closed. The kids all gathered around Mark. Mark slowly opened his fist, palm up. Everyone's eyes widened at the sight of the six shiny objects Mark was holding in his hand.

"Um, Billy. I don't think Mark is talking about baseball diamonds," a shocked Missy whispered.

Missy was right. And the Wild Bunch was about to embark on its third, unbelievable adventure of this exciting summer.

...........READ THE REST IN:
The Sawyer Diamonds Mystery

Printed in the United States
22673LVS00001B/298-435

9 780975 973707